Steve Gehrke

About the Author

NADINE SABRA MEYER is a winner of the 2005 National Poetry Series, selected by John Koethe. Her poems have won the New Letters Poetry Prize and a Pushcart Prize, and have appeared in many journals, including *Chelsea*, *Quarterly West*, *Pleiades*, *Notre Dame Review*, and the *North American Review*. She is completing her Ph.D. at the University of Missouri–Columbia; teaching at Seton Hall University; and living in New Jersey with her husband, poet Steve Gehrke, and their daughter, Chloe.

THE
ANATOMY
THEATER

The National Poetry Series was established in 1978 to ensure the publication of five poetry books annually through participating publishers. Publication is funded by the Lannan Foundation; the late James A. Michener and Edward J. Piszek through the Copernicus Society of America; Stephen Graham; International Institute of Modern Letters; Joyce and Seward Johnson Foundation; Juliet Lea Hillman Simonds Foundation; and the Tiny Tiger Foundation. This project also is supported in part by an award from the National Endowment for the Arts, which believes that a great nation deserves great art.

2005 OPEN COMPETITION WINNERS

Steve Gehrke of Columbia, Missouri, *Michelangelo's Seizure*
Chosen by T. R. Hummer, to be published by University of Illinois Press

Nadine Sabra Meyer of Columbia, Missouri, *The Anatomy Theater*
Chosen by John Koethe, to be published by Harper Perennial

Patricia Smith of Tarrytown, New York, *Teahouse of the Almighty*
Chosen by Edward Sanders, to be published by Coffee House Press

S. A. Stepanek of West Chicago, Illinois, *Three, Breathing*
Chosen by Mary Ruefle, to be published by Verse Press/Wave Books

Tryfon Tolides of Farmington, Connecticut, *An Almost Pure Empty Walking*
Chosen by Mary Karr, to be published by Penguin Books

THE ANATOMY THEATER

POEMS

NADINE SABRA MEYER

HARPER PERENNIAL

NEW YORK • LONDON • TORONTO • SYDNEY

HARPER ● PERENNIAL

NATIONAL
ENDOWMENT
FOR THE ARTS

HarperCollins books may be purchased for educational, business, or sales promotional use. For information please write: Special Markets Department, HarperCollins Publishers, 10 East 53rd Street, New York, NY 10022.

FIRST EDITION

Designed by Justin Dodd

Library of Congress Cataloging-in-Publication Data

Meyer, Nadine Sabra.
    The anatomy theater : poems / Nadine Sabra Meyer.— 1st Harper Perennial ed.
        p. cm.— (The national poetry series)
    ISBN-10: 0-06-112217-3
    ISBN-13: 978-0-06-112217-0
    I. Title. II. Series.
    PS3613.E975A83 2006
    811'.6—dc22   2005058165

06 07 08 09 10 ❖/RRD 10 9 8 7 6 5 4 3 2 1

for Steve Gehrke

CONTENTS

ACKNOWLEDGMENTS

The poems listed here have appeared or are forthcoming in the following journals, sometimes in earlier versions.

Chelsea: "For Those Floating Above Vitebsk" (sections 1–4 and 6)
CutBank: "At the Cirque Fernando: The Ringmaster"
Gulf Coast: "The Flayed Man"
MARGIE: "Driving Between Doctors" (from "The Paper House")
Mississippi Review: "Dancing at the Moulin Rouge"
New Letters: "Effigy of John Donne Wrapped in His Death Shroud," "Flap Anatomy," "The Hook" (from "The Paper House"), "Miss La La at the Circus," "The Gorgons," and "John Donne on His Deathbed"
The North American Review: "Klimt's Unfinished Bride" and "Over Vitebsk" (from "For Those Floating Above Vitebsk")
Notre Dame Review: "Man in a Field of Sunflowers" (sections 2 and 3)
Pleiades Magazine: "Dissection Prayers"
Quarterly West: "The Anatomy Theater" and "The Cadaver"
The Southern Poetry Review: "The Artist at the Dissection"
13th Moon: "January" and "This Strange Home" (from "The Paper House")
Washington Square: "Seasonal Incantation"

"The Flayed Man" is included in *The Pushcart Prize Anthology XXIX, 2005.*

I would like to thank Lynne McMahon and Sherod Santos for their insightful critiques of many of the poems in this book, as well as of the book as a whole; Jennifer Atkinson and Eric Pankey for their early support; and, especially, Steve Gehrke, whose intellectual drive challenged me to reconceive poems in this volume.

Thank you to *New Letters* for awarding me the New Letters Prize in Poetry 2005 for a group of poems from this book.

Who are these coming to the sacrifice?
To what green altar, O mysterious priest,
Lead'st thou that heifer lowing at the skies,
And all her silken flanks with garlands drest?

—John Keats "Ode on a Grecian Urn"

EFFIGY OF JOHN DONNE WRAPPED IN HIS DEATH SHROUD

. . . I am comming to that Holy roome,
Where, with thy Quire of Saints for evermore,
I shall be made thy Musique

When you had them swaddle you,
a baby in its death bunting, all slung bone,
elbow knobs, knee sockets, harp-bone
of your chest, you were, *yes,*
His music then, fired and kiln-baked,
sweating through your glaze, a ladder
of bones propped heavenward.
And when, Dean of St. Paul's, it burned
years later to its girders, flames flushing
London's streets, your death shroud
making you a pillar with no limbs
to crack in the fall, the lineaments
of your emaciation burned through
cerements of stone as if within
a marble mantel lay your living form.
Yours was the only of the cathedral's effigies
found later, somehow unscathed, pardoned
and laid on your side in the choir's charred throat.
Within the cathedral's fevered frame,
its rib-timbers scorched and trembling,
crash and plunder, organ-song, you were,

again, His music, this blessed torment
for which He pulls out all the stops
and draws from a soul petrified in stone
steeple–hue, bell–clap, sun glint in split glass.

I.

THE FLAYED MAN

after Juan de Valverde's 1560 anatomy text, Anatomia del corpo umano

He has flayed himself for our inspection, pressed
his knife through the dermis of his large right toe,
run its tip along the base of his foot, splitting left
from right, up the back of his calf and thigh, carefully,
the way a woman runs the seam of her stockings
up the midline of each leg, and slipped his muscled
and gelatinous body from its casing. As one slices
the skin from an apple in a long spiraling similitude,
he has kept, where possible, his ghostly likeness
intact. In one hand he holds it out to us, a testament
to what he's done, and in the other he holds
the knife. Martyr for science, he stands, each muscle
overdeveloped, numbered for the anatomist's study
as if it were possible to slit this human casing, slip
from one's integument and go on living
in the delicate inner flesh. What then is beauty
when the skin has been shucked? A marbling of muscle
and fat, the patterning of veins and arteries, tenderness
of disease? Complicit, a participant in his own dissection,
the Flayed Man brandishes his life: without regard
for his soul, he offers this oblation, his own decorticated
corpus, to Medicine and Anatomy. For over a thousand
years, for fear that to dissect the body impedes

the soul's chrysalis, its incorporeal unfurling, the study
of anatomy had virtually stopped, but now
the Flayed Man, his jaunty disregard, his terrible
theatrical privation, the outstretched offering
of his own skin as if to say, *all this, I have done for you.*

THE ANATOMY THEATER

after a wood-block print in Andreas Vesalius's De humani corporis fabrica, *1543*

Do they strain to see the glimmer of a soul rise,
two souls like a pair of dusty starlings?
Or is it the visceral they are interested in, this great
concourse of arms and legs and heads thronging
toward the center of the amphitheater, where,
at its vortex, a woman, the only stillness,
has, like a peach dropped in boiling water,
split down her gravid center? The rabble jockeys
toward her womb; men press through the balcony
bars, gesture largely, scrabble to touch the cloth
she lies on, a bit of thigh, or the back of the anatomist's
cape. The anatomist, a magician in his dark robes,
his prostrate lady before him, looks out at us
(what secret will he withdraw next? the veined
balloon of her bladder, the umber stalk
of the umbilicus, the fetus's tiny froglike foot?)
and raises a finger to bid us *attend*. But it is the skeleton
who presides over this carnival; he sits
on the balcony railing, dead center, staff in hand.
He is regal and captive amid the gaiety, at the site
of his own dissection: this room to which bodies
stolen from the gallows are brought and are made
to play their final role, organ by organ, this room which,

with its hyaline dome where at night the stars
of the firmament ring, mimics heaven.
The skeleton turns his fixed grimace toward
the vaulted ceiling, its refulgent cupola
and lambent mahogany beams. Does his soul still swim
in the stippled air, among the steam of gold pieces rising
from the open womb of the newly dead: a mosaic
of ovum and gilded spermatozoa? Is the rotunda's
cylinder of air teeming even now with colorful bits
of the dead rattling against its diaphanous dome?

DISSECTION PRAYERS

after Andreas Vesalius

Incised by one long meridian,
    the cadaver is broken
down the spine, and what glistens
    in the rift,
in the constellation of unfastened
    flesh is nature's text,
which Vesalius reads
    like Braille.
The living would give anything,
    it seems,
to know what the dead know,
    to lift the pall
of flesh and find more than a charnel house,
    a strung charm
of bone. The anatomist learned
    to articulate
the skeleton, to string it
    with wire, and so
make a pageantry of death,
    the laboratory
an exalted theater where,
    galvanized

by an iron vein run down
        the spinal column,
each manikin became an unlikely
        figurehead for God.
He saw, in the lovely
        interlock
of bone, in these man-sized
        amulets, a heavenly
coherence. But what form
        of praise is this:
while saying twenty masses
        as required by law
for the souls of those
        dissected,
he searches in the viscera
        of the cadaver,
uprooting the vena cava,
        the mushrooming
uterus, the dark cabbage
        of a heart?
If, with a moth flutter, the spirit
        escapes (or
perishes), then what a charade,
        pickpocketing

the organs of the condemned.
        And what grand larceny
if Vesalius had, in fact,
        firked out
the soul from the body's loam.
        Believing that hanging
paid for their sins, the condemned
        on the way
to the gallows still prayed
        their bodies not
be pilfered, their anatomies
        made public,
souls clipped by the first incision,
        the mind a nest of eels
unraveling in the anatomist's hands.
        Standing on the platform,
each below his own hemp circlet,
        their prayers
are the susurrations of the cicada
        sloughing its shell.

THE CADAVER

after Jean Riolan's Les oeuvres anatomiques, *1629*

He lies on his side, hips stacked, chest thrown
back, chin thrust forward as in waking, as if,
after his lover has seen to his lovely body
on the white sheets, he will rise and,
with the quivering firefly of his cigarette,
move nude through the predawn kitchen.
But his abdomen has been split, penis
to sternum, and an anatomist opens the lips
of his wound. He has been given a second sex,
as if to slit and enter the body were fundamentally
sexual. His cock lies gently across one thigh,
his great new sex opens across his abdomen.
A team of anatomists works over this man, rendered
delicate in his androgyny, hips narrow as a boy's,
ankles clasped in prayer. Their hands rest
on his flank and buttocks, point to his innards.
They surround the table and the man with the beautiful
open body who, in the text's dream, lives in a world
where he will rise from under this caress
and the cooking smoke from his eggs
and bacon will blend with that of his cigarette.
The skin over his thorax is delicate; you can make out

the constellation of dark hairs, the dark stars of his nipples.
His face is startled, in this wood-block print,
in pleasure as he faces his own death, his soul's
rendezvous, or is it in climax, the anatomists' hands
low on his belly where his two sexes meet?

FLAP ANATOMY

after an anonymous seventeenth-century figurine

You can open her like a locket,
spring the clasp at her side, spread
her tiny silver hinge; her ivory
navel, a delicate porcelain flap
contrived to reveal and hide
her perpetual gestation, peels back
like a doll-sized dryer door,
a fetus rolling in the drum of her
ceramic cavity. An exquisite idol,
a gravid Buddha, she stands
forever frozen in expectancy.
Her breasts must ache, surely
her ankles swell, and the weight
on her spine's unbearable, though she's
serene and formal—uterus cleft
by the jeweler's saw, thighs pinned shut.
Immortal ivory icon, Goddess of Fertility,
your whiteness is alabaster; how can you bear
the curator's incubator, this world
controlled by the thermostat's click?
Here, where atmosphere retards
change, it might take nine centuries
to deliver! Beneath your glass dome,

do you pray to crack first, to turn
to grains fine as salt? Woman,
your crystalline sphere is museum glass,
what you take for the firmament,
track lighting; they have made
of you a specimen, exotic plague
under glass, as if your abdomen
were Pandora's box and you carry
pestilence in your dowry-locked womb,
but dignified, elegant, the way
a mother wears her child at her throat,
you've borne yours three centuries in your
locket womb, its door ajar as if, if our eyes
were good enough, we might see on the belly
in your womb a tiny-*tiny* clasp and hinge.

APOLLO AND MARSYAS

after Andreas Vesalius's De humani corporis fabrica, *1543*

What melody rises from the satyr's throat,
as Apollo, tender as a father unzipping
his infant's suit, slits down Marsyas's thorax?
Naked, Marsyas's man-body gleams;
arms raised over his head, he is bound,
like a woman to a headboard, his wrists to a tree.
God of music, God of healing, why
string out the flesh note by brutal note?
At his feet: his flute divested, and his cloak,
rumpled and fragrant, lies like flesh,
the cloth sloughed from a babe.
Apollo wears his signature laurel,
the crown of thorns he braided of Daphne:
a symbol of mourning, he claims, though
the nymphs think it vengeance. They know
that in life, when Daphne refused him
the circumference of her body, in death
he wrought her to ring him, twining
her limbs in his hair and lyre. Like a tree
scalded and cleft to the root, a *V*, and all
the feminine retribution it suggests
is splayed across this landscape. Though here,

in this illuminated anatomy text, the *V*
is also for Vesalius who, like Apollo, flays humanity
for its crimes. The impropriety of scavenging
bodies is eclipsed by this strange alliance
and Vesalius vindicated. In the *V*'s crux,
an earlier scene: Marsyas and Apollo,
small as putti, playing the flute and lyre.
With what pastoral innocence this grisly scene
is portrayed, and look, the Muses, their lovely
abdomens bared, serve as tribunal and approve
this punishment, the skinning of Marsyas alive
like a pomegranate! Meticulously performing
this ritual undressing, his knife, a zipper's tab
glinting steadily in the sun, Apollo is Marsyas's
conductor and draws from him all the crushed music
agony demands. Marsyas's pain choruses,
his harmony stretches from knife to kneecap,
and Apollo's blade, sharper than a lyre's pick,
plays a sweeter sound, as the buzzards overhead
braid the air with jealousy, that their rude throats
might render such song. When Vesalius lowers
the swollen fruit from the trees and the crossbows

of the gallows, he imagines a Muse's breath
in each ear, the blessing of knowledge ringing
his head like a laurel, for he like Apollo, divining
music from string and shell, distills,
from the stench of flesh, pure thought.

THE ARTIST AT THE DISSECTION

after Stephan Kalkar's anatomical prints, De humani corporis fabrica, *1543*

Sometimes he draws them prone
and vacated, flaccid beyond sleep,
moving already toward dissolution
as thoughts decompose under anesthesia,
then cease to exist—that uncanny silence
we think mimics death. But there,
if all goes well, the mind is resurrected,
the body returns to its habits of breath
and blood, the quiver of small motors
under the skin. Here, in Vesalius's
makeshift laboratory, the converted barn
where each morning the sun assails cadavers
strung up like bushels of tobacco leaves
drying from the rafters, there is no returning
to these bodies, their strata of flesh, the organs
that filled the strange wings of their pelvises.
At other times he draws them animate, experts
of their own bodies: a woman, stepping down
from a pedestal, removes her uterus,
exhibits its size and shape; a skeleton,
leaning on a podium, gestures with a skull
and lectures on the bones of the body.
What is it to say the body, dressing

and undressing itself, can instruct us?
Or that, for our edification, the dead
willingly model their once insular selves
made plural? A man thrusts two fingers
through the flesh below his navel,
where once his lover circled her palm,
and tears, the horizontal gash flowering intestine;
another, having torn back the cornhusk
of his flesh, offers the veins of his forearm.
Our predecessors have returned to be our preceptors;
expecting the mysteries of the macrocosm,
they have had instead revealed to them
those of the microcosm, the infinities
of the body which they flaunt and shimmy
before us: look, the Muscle Men have stepped
from their fleshy membranes and wear
their lovely muscles loose on their frames,
as if each had worked his whole life to be in death
a perfect specimen. Quadriceps ribboning
their thighs, pectorals twisted
in elegant knots, they lift their faces
to the sun. But the anatomist
aids decomposition, and in each

successive plate he ravages
their supplicant forms, stripping them
of superficial muscle and denuding
the interior, so that the superhuman
unravel and slabs of flesh hang viscous.
Our disciples, despoiled and pillaged,
have become macabre, indeed, but perhaps
this grisly elegy—this ascension
from the grave to the artist's chisel—
is the only there is; witness the skeleton
digging himself from the grave to stand before
Kalkar's cartographic gaze that he might have
what is mortal immortalized. This, at least,
is what the artist tells himself: *The dead come willingly*,
though too often the specter of his first dissection
rises into his dreams: the exhumed body
laid out on the dissecting table, Vesalius
throwing his weight against the heavy cord,
the gears of a pulley fixed to the rafters grinding
to life like the great misshapen blades of a fan,
the marionette, hauled to a seated position
by the bones of its face, lurching dementedly
from the table, its feet momentarily planted

on the dirt floor as if struggling to stand,
and then, quickened by this inverse hanging,
the bedlamite—his head and torso jangling—
is hoisted from the barn floor
into the light that rends the granular air.

II.

SEASONAL INCANTATION

I. AUTUMN SONG

As the sun unrolls the belt of its ecliptic, tail-fire ticker tape,
the moon, pig fat and wax, pares itself down to pith.

Adam and Eve are solemn as eggplants,
ingenuous, each, as cucumber and sunflower.

Her belly's a snow globe, a glassy microcosm, encasing
the rings of the planets, fixed stars and heavenly sphere.

A paper-thin Christ, he's lean as the universe, gears
and ligatures, transparent, spacious.

Where his skin falls away, the rivers of a forearm,
heartland of his thigh, foot engorged in flame-root.

All year long the tawny haired witch drags
the tarot pack of her wake across our bodies.

This earth is star-seed fruit, cross-sectioned
and pitted in divinations of four.

She shines, as through a hole in a church roof,
and pricks her way across my foot, calf and groin.

Echo of bullfrog, bow resin on strings, catgut and heart
tremor, the kidney is crosshatch, is snare.

In throb and leaf rot, the wheels of fortune
unwind their hieroglyphs, their long proclamation:

*. . . amputation saw, raven's beak,
varnished human arteries in cedar wood . . .*

My throat is cornhusk. My heart is partitioned in four.
My hand is memory, is magic.

My hand is the pelican's foot:
attenuated muscle in bone-claw.

My body is a silhouette of chalk dust,
it's a paper doll cutout with pencil-thin scars.

No, it's frog heart and frog lung, Nadine,
sheep spleen and cow liver, clotted as milk and blood-sour.

II. SUMMER SONG

In summer we molt six times, skin thin as tracing paper,
the marrow of our bones sweet clotted cream.

The cherry tree warns of fevers and vomiting,
rise of the Dogstar, ache of the turtledove.

We spin the wheel of health, the pregnancy calendar,
index finger to the moon.

Impermeable septum, membrane about the heart,
we are cloudy and granulous, suspended with plaque.

We doctor us with flint and friction, fool's gold,
the cabbage's waxy leaves, the radish's brass sting.

From the brains of Jupiter, the learned Minerva came forth,
while we are spittle and salt.

We carry between us the urinal basket of our bodies.
The medical month is twenty-six days.

When our elements are wild as kettle steam,
to zinc-flint and copper-flakes, we add philosopher's stone.

The dromedary carries, in its two body flasks,
a blessing for each dry cell.

Deep in the starry gum of our pituitary glands, our souls
are mercury, sulfur and salt.

They are the sum of the angles of the triangle, together
we make a full wheel.

Our love is alchemy, strange cure-all.
We heat seed the color of permanence.

Our bodies are pressed coal, thin as ash,
they ring like tin.

The body is warlock, the body is sorceress,
and we are alchemists: *look what we made from dross.*

From our one fluid—blood, urine, milk,
sperm—the crowning first crow.

Summer is solstice. Our blood is the color of the sea.
Our hours are saffron, they are leek-green.

III. ATHENA'S SPRING RANT

It was I who gave him the shield, I
who burnished it with my knitting wool

until, like the Aegean at midday, it showed my face
as in a silver coin.

His physique is cut for hero worship, it's true,
and holding her head,

snaked with curls, aloft,
knife of his groin, he makes a fine statue.

But when he held the shield before her like a looking glass,
and, like a two-faced whore, it

torqued his gaze, it was I
who guided his hand to her neck-quiver.

Without me, he'd have cleaved air from air,
nicked a serpent awake, his heart slowing

to agate, his lips freezing to rose quartz, elongated feet
and his cock to sandstone.

From the mulberry tree, the west wind breathed
madness, bloody flux, melancholia,

and a body, tender as mine, lies on mountain crag,
its neck truncated and pearled in fly-sheen.

They said we were women of equal beauty, elegant
as reed-fronds swaying the pond's ringed surface,

alike as Narcissus and the watery man who rose
from the pond to meet him.

But I was born from the head of Zeus,
and she is all cunt.

With Neptune, king of underwater, she profaned
my temple, my hallowed vault, my long white columns,

so I drew from her the excrement of her act
and crowned her in her own maggots.

Then, as I knew he would, Perseus became inflamed,
for what man can stand, in a woman, such visceral ugliness?

Slag from the alchemist's vat, coal flecks in diamond,
she is the dregs of my spirit, my lower half, terra to my empyrean.

I have drawn numbers, like stars from a well,
and arranged them for both men and gods to use.

I discovered body armor, the four-horse chariot, weapons of iron.
Named for me there is a citadel, a city, a people.

If I could, I'd lose this body altogether.
If I could, I'd slay the stars;

instead I hold my aegis against the grim face of disease,
for I have made Medusa Queen of the Body.

Her horrible carnality wards off the carnal,
let her suffer its paroxysm.

She is what should lie veiled, grotesque mask, my mirror-face.
I have made her my amulet, my lucky-piece, evil-eye, my fetish.

See: I have stamped her into my shield, bright
as the Aegean when it lies flat and is blue with the sky.

IV. WINTER SONG

Body fitted to mine, husk to my kernel,
the olive tree bares its fruit of salt and sex.

We are leaden as the cormorant's cry,
a blade across the horizon, ash on water.

Slate sea and shale sediment, it is by deposition
and erosion, we become the earth's crust.

I love the iron of this earth pressed into my bones,
its silvery tacks, the steel nail curled about my finger.

Deep in its molten forge, in its volcanic throat,
we are the smithy's poker.

Tongue-metal red, you burn and scar.
I am a slab of sulfur.

The coin-faced sun thunders the sky over our rib ties,
our heart racket, bone clamor, cardiac shudder.

The moon is all but gone now.
When I move, I leave a shadow, a veined inner self.

The townsfolk don't need us.
They have their rituals of seed and harvest.

But don't trust the earth-pit,
this soil is rich with scapulae and vertebrae.

Don't spill the vial of your melancholy,
for below the dregs, it is calibrated with death.

Let us draw well water, your foot planted in wheat-husk,
mine in marl, residue of metals on our tongues.

Let us sauté peppers green as autumn
and yellow as our youth.

. . . *tongue of calyx, blood of pomegranate,*
kiwi's hoary skin . . .

We will capture your urine, amber-bright
and running from you like tree sap.

It will settle, like the universe,
to sediment, suspension and nebula.

We will read it like Galen at his decanters,
like God at the world's incunabula.

We will draw calendars for your bloodletting, and, love,
we will leech you with strong warm mouths.

THE PAPER HOUSE

Mourning doves score the telephone wires,
three rumps, tails aslant:

bird, space, space, bird, space, bird.

What iconography against the silent heavens!
To work and back, you carry something sick and invisible

woven into your side: a mesh bag.
A sudden clarifying of your hip bone. Porous sky.

The doves carry on in silence, their feathers trill, nervous bird-glance.
What do they read in this sky thick as gauze?

In two hands, you carry yourself to doctors,
offering up the body on a metal table, a steel shelf, a plate.

You lay out the thing sick and invisible,
and they look at you like you're beautiful.

❊   ❊   ❊

He must have entered me the way you open an orange,
catch your blade in the navel,
press your thumb through its resistance: two neat slits
no more than half an inch in length,

but my blood must have risen to the surface
like that of no fruit.
He had emphasized his respect
for the body's integrity, his desire
to keep the organs intact whenever possible.
Now, I too am fascinated by the integrity of the body,
the way it stands up after injury,
and by the way this man
could go unflinchingly through my abdomen
as my brother, in his five-year-old wisdom,
could reach down a fish's gullet,
work out the hook
where it had caught in intimate flesh, then raise the fish,
glistening and triumphant, up over his head,
each bone in his little-boy body visible,
as he bent
and let it flicker away.

❉   ❉   ❉

I don't know if it was a dream, but I remember
during surgery a woman's voice saying, *She has a pretty body naked*,
and there were hands rubbing my body back to life,

wrapping me in warm towels, another voice saying,
You can tell she exercises, a blessed numbing salve between my legs,
and my doctor's voice, *I could feel the muscles of her abdomen*

as I went in, and then, as I struggled to surface,
the first voice again, *Her breasts are very cystic,*
perhaps there is something there, too.

❁   ❁   ❁

What is it like for these men
who open a window in a woman's breast

and carefully cut out the mass?
In the exam room, his wrist rests on your hip,

the other hand gently probes your breast.
Part father, part lover, he shows you

where he'll cut along the edge of the nipple
then tenderly closes your paper shirt.

He takes your hand in both of his
and kisses your cheek before leaving,

this man who will open your body.
When he goes home at night

to his wife and puts his hands on her hips,
her breasts, how does he keep from thinking of that

which lies under her skin, loosening with age?
Or is it easy, slipping under her skin

knowing both the body's promise and its retreat?

❈　　　　　❈　　　　　❈

I have been thinking
How the body would crush easily

Against the driveshaft, under a telephone pole,
Any strange happening.

The pelvis crushes easily as a walnut, more easily,
The organs' delicacy unprotected,

Cupped in a half shell:
This strange home.

A stroke went off in his brain,
And he, who to you never did, spoke in French.

Low-flying planes rattle the window frames,
And the geese are calling a convention on the lake.

Qu'est-ce que c'est?
We walk upright in our slug bodies, luminous.

❁   ❁   ❁

 Driving between doctors I carry my ovary in my purse,
an anomalous globe, the size and color of a hen's egg,

but this ovoid mass is spotted with imperfections—
red stains of endometrium mar its white tissue.

Holding it in pink folds of flesh, my abdominal cavity is itself marked,
and in the next frame, close up, a cul-de-sac of blood-fluid.

I carry my photograph like a prize,
taking it out at stoplights

to examine the anomalous egg, the veined tissue.
Taken during surgery, my photo is more clear

than the sonogram of any forming fetus,
this familiar organ as visible as the hand

that holds it, and the source of my pain evident
after all these months.

A fish carries its eggs loose in its side, a spider
in a sticky mesh bag.

This struggling white mass,
I would take up in my mouth and care for.

III.

AT THE CIRQUE FERNANDO
THE RINGMASTER

It is the horse's ass that catches your eye,
enormous beneath the tail, brushed like a girl's,
to a platinum shine. But the girl on this
circus pony is a redhead; her ass,
perched sidesaddle on the horse's flank,
and the sash at her waist, knotted
in glimmering wings, promise flight.
Next you notice the Ringmaster, his eyes
trained on the girl, her eyes on his, the rope
of their gazes more palpable than
the whip powering the pony's stride.
He, in his double-breasted suit,
will conduct her flight, her explosion
from the horse's heft, her body tearing
through the clown's papered hula hoop.
The horse, its charged cargo on its back,
races in a hectic arc, where
a clown atop a painted stool raises
a new full moon each time the velum O
is ruptured, as though each time were her first,
and the men who squat in stadium seating
see her, again and again, in her first throws,
like the girls who dance at the Moulin Rouge

where Toulouse-Lautrec first learned illusion,
the clamshell undersides of skirts, the way
they'd dance and twist, frenzied as ponies.
He painted them with wild energy
in their skirts, though their faces were
composed as stone, their eyes detached: a blouse
like any aristocrat's, a hat with plume,
but legs you couldn't focus on and, beneath,
the purple snatches of their underthings.
She's like, too, the *femmes de maison*
who each time they'd take him in, would arch
and tense as though he were their first. But painter
of lightning skirts and bombed-out eyes, he must
have known each time the woman swayed and groaned
she disappeared through the darkness at the center
of her mind. Each time she breaks the barrier,
Fernando's girl lands with ease on the horse's
rolling muscle. The clowns, with sleight of hand,
swiftly dispose of all those rings, but in the circus
memory, in the sphere's stale air, there hangs
the absence of a girl, her shadow space,
her body's tear in each discarded moon.

THE UNFINISHED BRIDE

She is rising from the canvas body first:
oval of her navel, pink circles of her nipples,
torso narrow as a doll's, thighs apart
beneath her ornate skirt only partly there,
as if this is the way she surfaced into his thoughts,
a body wiry and forthright, rising
into the developing tray of his imagination.
After his death, she hung on the wall
of his studio, half-made, like a fetus
in its amphibian formlessness,
only her most private parts fully articulated
beneath the gossamer skirt: a girl
caught in the act of dressing.
How many paintings did Klimt begin this way,
with the woman's body frank and naked
on the canvas? After decades under the museum's
bright lights, perhaps the paint begins to slough,
and Adele Bloch-Bauer, one of Vienna's nouveaux riches,
begins her strange striptease: first a craze of cracks
across her bodice, the surface of her dress
like the ice-scrim on a lake, then the alluvial flaking.
This, then, is Klimt's argument for the supremacy
of the body, its ability to burn through any concealment.
He painted Adele's face last as he would have

the girl he left when he died, strange,
shapeless scratchings where her face should be
and, stretched across her doll-hips, a fabric of sexual glistenings,
the skirt-silk bleeding out into the starred web of spirit,
and Klimt, had he lived, like an apothecary over his glass,
would have bent, dipped his brush into the cordial
of her body, withdrawn the drops of spirit and let them fall,
an oily tincture across the surface of the face.
Don't you see? This canvas is a sonogram: here
we see the pulse of the self drawing into being
this liminal specter, ghost-limbed,
on the brink of the quickening wash.

THE ARTIST AT HIS CANVAS

Risen from sleep he stands
naked before the canvas,
which looks back at him frankly
as he wields his pallet knife
in a vague paranoid flourish.
His skin is colorless as the sheets
he's strewn like a drop cloth
across the hardwood, except where,
from an unseen window, the moon
has spilt milk across his chest
and bicep, as if it were here,
in the anemic glow of the body, deep
in the pupil-dark of each cell,
that thought originates: his head hoary
and disheveled as his genitals,
his nipples alert in the slack moon-pearled skin,
as the artist's right arm lifts him
from sleep and draws him here
to the window of his canvas so that
we see him exposed unabashedly,
only his shoes flapping on his feet.

AT THE SALON OF 1865

What voyeurism is this? We have stumbled upon
this room in which a woman, laid out on a silky
bourgeois bed, wears at her neck, though she's
otherwise nude, a ribbon, knotted, and, from a wrist-cuff,
a quivering teardrop emerald. She receives us, here,
in the chiaroscuro of her private room, as she might
in her drawing room, though her lips are
a bit pursed, her expression drawn.
From the darkness, her servant woman
approaches with an armful of— Are those
flowers? What will they do with them?
Oh, put them about the house, I suppose,
but isn't this an inopportune moment?
The lady of the house is clearly entertaining. Her eyes,
on us, are cool as pennies and confrontational
as though we are an expected, though unpleasant, intrusion.
And intrude we do, though this closeted scene
must be for our benefit. Why else does this Venus look
so directly at us, one hand coyly covering her lap,
the other fingering an occidental drape? Her African
maid eyes her questioningly; she is darkness
in Christian linen, white as her lady's skin.
She offers the flowers still wrapped in paper
from the market, the way her lady offers us her body,

and at the foot of their bed a black cat eyes us all
from the whites of his eyes. Whose dream is this,
the equation so simple, the cat's tail rising like smoke?
If beneath each middle-class woman's starched beauty,
beneath the luster of her moon-bathed skin, beneath that hand
lies something known to the woman so dark
she hasn't a face, known to their feral minion,
then it's no surprise riots broke out and guards
were needed. But when the critics threatened
to throw stones at her, tearing through
the canvas of her flesh, at whom was this anger
directed? At Manet, who had held up a vision
like that in each wife's looking glass? At his intimation
that beneath each wife's white flesh lay a servant girl:
occult, foreign, diseased? Or was it at this woman herself,
the working-class girl, who had lain for him, looked him
directly in the eye, knowing precisely the cost?

MISS LA LA AT THE CIRCUS

Hauled by her teeth gripping a tiny trapeze,
a triangle better suited for the brassy ring
of cavorting clowns who play to her assent
the handbell, cymbal-clash and tambourine,

she's a pencil's line, she thinks, drawn
with precision up the rotunda's spine:
the tapering ribbon of her ponytail
and her ballet shoes stencil a silky line.

Miss La La knows she's a fish impaled
on a tinsel hook, her garish scales
shivering the brook of circus light,
but, with an elephant on a monocycle,

and a tiger straight from Cairo,
she's proud she's the woman strung
in sequined skin from ceiling beams who
each night makes the crowd come undone.

Nearing the ceiling's artificial jungle, its plantains
and coconut groves, she pikes, arabesques and releases
the bit so that, no net, from rings to trapeze,
she's safe in the arc of each parabola, in the dense

architecture she builds, towers, parts
the backlit air, so that castles, battlement, spires
upsurge in her wake, and beneath a heaven colonized,
Miss La La spells in flight the drama of our hearts.

THE GORGONS

Snakes, gold as the amulets his father
engraved for Vienna's rich, writhe
in the Gorgons' hair, coil and nest
like splendid ornaments. Raven
as the rims of their eyes, obsidian
as the sea of conception,
their tresses shroud their shoulders
and breasts, leaving the long stretch
of their bodies white silica.
Not the water nymphs Klimt dipped
in glistening stars of algae, these
anemic muses, haunted and ashen,
wear nothing but their feral eyes,
a patch of dry hair. Disease, Madness
and Death, their horrible sterility
evident, must be victims of some sexual
holocaust: snakes hobbling their wrists
and ankles, flesh porous as wasps' nests.
They are handsome and pliant
as all young women Klimt painted,
but this time he saw in each model's belly,
white as the underside of mackerel,
the tender quiver of pain, and painted
the body's secret into each searing visage.

In legend the Gorgons are hideous and powerful,
scales of impenetrable epithelium,
but perhaps this, as Klimt painted it, is what it is
to be woman, wincing and plagued, Athena
having turned you to beast that all men might dream
of your slaying, of carrying your head
home, as Perseus did, by the threads
of your hair. Is this our torture, the curse
Athena wrought on these sisters who dared
be beautiful: in the hollow of the pelvis,
a nest with two raised heads, alert and hissing?

HYGIEIA

Goddess of health is a diva; part sorceress,
part woman in bondage, she wears
the vestiges of slavery as ornament.
Jawbone to clavicle she is bound
in a gold-link chain inlaid with onyx,
and her wrists clatter with bangles,
with the delicate reminiscence of shackles.
Her bearing is that of high priestess;
chin raised, lovely features swollen
with paint, she turns her back on humanity
and feeds her snake from a glass bowl.
Gold as the embroidery of her red silk,
her snake coils one forearm, arches
and drops its head into the bowl she raises
like a torch, sending bubbles of light,
mystic, erotic, boiling across the canvas.
Prima donna, coquette of the twentieth
century, why this broad drama?
What happened to our modest woman
in sandals, the Hygieia with the power
and proclivity to heal? Now, more
snake charmer than woman healer,
has Hygieia's power been so usurped
that she must play at this false wizardry?

How many women have turned to this
grand display—the femme fatale
flaunting her power to deny, to reject,
to ruthlessly cut off? But Hygieia knows
drawing a snake from the embroidery
of her dress is no magic
compared with the plain white rags
she'd tear from her skirts for healing.
Behind her, humanity, tangled
as in a mass grave, is cowed and forsaken.
Forced to live in the corporeal, shade
collecting in the bowls of their eyes,
under the shelves of their cheekbones,
even the young are marked
by signs of death, even the most
vigorous is prelude to the skeleton.
Only Hygieia is bodiless, for she is clothed
in the garish exotic silks of aristocracy,
as if perfect health is to live, somehow,
blessed without a body. When,
at the start of the twentieth century,
Hygieia bent, as she always had,
to rinse her rag in the stream
and turned again toward humanity,

she found it a mass of naked bodies
washed away from her, the muscular,
the dead and the desiccated in a living embrace,
and that Medicine, in search of a symbol,
had, for its caduceus, stolen her living snake.

DANCING AT THE MOULIN ROUGE

I. 1895

      Fevered in her art, drumming
         in her skirt's layers
of shimmering organza, she has lost
         the subtlety of youth,
the waiflike innocence
         which pretends
the body is ornament,
         a trinket to jostle
and splay, light as a plastic ring
         spun across the bar
between forefinger and thumb.
         Although her leading man
dances easily as well as she,
         he's disappearing, the mere
suggestion of a man; Toulouse-Lautrec
         has painted him blending
into the air about them
         as if all that lasts
is motion, the broad-stroke sweep,
         the pendulous moon
pounding everything to Lautrec's
         unpainted night.
Only she is aging into solidity,
         determinedly

becoming more herself, as if her body, rejecting
    the dancer's illusion
of floating weightless, has clarified
    and become more palpable,
so that she is the painting's anchor,
    its black hole
collapsing all matter into itself:
    the shadowy crowd, the bulbs
wavering like balloons, even the painter who,
    sitting just beyond
the painting's frame, was sidekick
    to the main attraction,
peripheral even in the center of his life, an eye
    through which to view
a degraded world, ferocious carnival.
    Hunched before the cardboard
set on his easel, his bones unrolling bolts
    of sheet lightning across
his consciousness, pain spitting
    down his spine, he felt himself pulled
apart cell by cell, his brush sucked
    always to the woman's vortex

so that her skin became thick and white
    as the rest of the dance hall seemed
to loosen and fly apart and he,
    like the leading man, thinned
to transparency as if already, even
    in the reverberating barroom,
he was an apparition, the silhouette
    of a man in a doorway
in the moment just after he's left.

II. 1890

Her legs, two clappers
in the bell of her dress,
as a girl she'd careen
the dance-hall floor,
the men swinging
like lanterns into her sight,
the band's syncopated
thunder loosening her joints,
playing her like a puppet
so that she became
a dummy of a girl
jimmied to the thrumming beat
of the salon's suspiration.
In the center of his canvas,
Lautrec caught
in sparkler strokes, beneath
her dun-colored dress,
its lightning-white
underside, her silky offering.
He painted in this ring
of flirty underthings
a suggestion that she
become the flip side

of her self, as if,
if turned inside out,
a girl would be
all shimmering phallus.
But dancer at the Moulin Rouge,
she's paid to epitomize woman,
and Lautrec has painted
her as a wick catacombed
in a candle, her sex glowing
eerily through the lampshade
of her skirt. Once
as a child, my sister took
a flashlight in her mouth,
and I watched as she became
a human lantern, a death's-
head, the opaque bones outlined
through translucent flesh. Now,
I know the body's vacant
as a jack-o'-lantern,
a place for hollow promises,
a clown's baggy suit,
the empty space behind
a carnival facade.

IV.

MAN IN A FIELD OF SUNFLOWERS

I.

It is an ordinary photograph: children,
trying to smile for the camera, grimace into the sun.

It is overexposed and more white than black,
their features difficult to discern. On the back is written *Été 1939*.

Nothing in the photograph intimates fear
or that these children will scatter.

They have been gathered from their play.
My father claps a ball against his hip.

His sister, Eliane, is playful, posing, leaning on her cousin, Paule.
Paule and Jeanine sit obediently, their faces upraised.

In the foreground is a toy car.
Under the stairs, a chicken coop.

The adults will bury their life savings under its back left corner,
and will show their children, telling them, *Remember this*.

As the children play, their parents make plans
to hide in small towns or to get visas or perhaps

they make dinner: boil potatoes, scrape carrots.
The steam that rises from the vegetables

hovers over the stove and collects on all of the faces.

2 .

Forty years after the war
my father went back
for the first time. His wife
tells me that, in a train station
just over the Spanish border
where, until some years back,
the French and Spanish lines met, to him
things became suddenly familiar.
First he remembered passengers
and freight being moved across the strip
from French to Spanish trains, but it was
the central cupola
where his mother
was strip-searched by Spaniards
that made the whole glass
and iron structure familiar, and he,

asking to be alone,
walked the length of the last station,
where at thirteen he lost
his father, his country, his friends
and small cousins,
got on a boat that took him to New York City,
met my mother and did his part
in repopulating the earth.

3.

His new wife must have asked him
To go into that field and stand
Between the sunflowers
Large as dinner plates, and he,
Packed seed and soft-petaled acquiescence,
Must have obliged out of love
And tender folly. She
Must have seen him
As unabashed heart
Offered up in two hands.
The ebullient sky overhead and everywhere
The sunflowers, tattered children about his hips.

FOR THOSE FLOATING ABOVE VITEBSK

I.

In Vitebsk the rainspouts drink to the sky, the spires,
like bottles of perfume,

scent the air with copper and bell song.
The lampposts are crooked matchsticks,

the chimney pots repentant sinners,
and all the town's fence posts line the heart's thoroughfare.

There is a Jew over Vitebsk tonight and no one to see him off,
though he carries his satchel, his cane and his hat,

and when he returns his paintings will be blackout curtains
under a fire-plumed sky: thunder in the heart-socket,

treble of the aspen trees, windows appalled by the skulls
shimmering in the reflections at their feet, and everywhere he goes,

this Jew who wanders, he carries with him these dimpled rooftops,
the gray fabric of this sky, and a soul which fills as it fills.

II.

Heart of a luminary, soul of a performer, you dance high as our opera
     balcony
with your one human eye.

With the face of a rooster, body of a woman, on your back, like a
     crucifix,
you wear great wings.

You fly high over our red shtetl, which spins like the world on its tip
and throbs like the liver of a gutted deer.

Red-handed, you flash the heritage of your clock, you reveal
the fiddler who plays like a drum on the field of your leotard,

and, like a celebration, you throw a leg in the air:
five fat toes, one lime ballet shoe.

The tulips wear feathers on their fingertips,
the dark auditorium sings with the dead,

and, in the audience, a man wears the moon smeared
in his hair,

as though Fortune were this phantasm in tights and we, high
like the moon in our parapet, her proselytes.

In the plums of our mouths, in the canals of our hearts,
a cardinal rattles its feathered frame

to you who dance on the wheel of the earth. But body of scarlet
jubilation, your cartwheel is loosening its spoke from rim,

so that, Donkey, your bride is in mourning, the ballerina in blue
drops her veil of rice across the stage of the earth,

which rolls in the ball of itself like an egg in its nest,
like a serpent coiled in a buzzard craw,

and, like a scarf drawn from the pocket of a dead man, the village
        bleeds
its stubborn turkey heart.

III.

Woman, from your skirts canaries fly.
Each day your face, high as our bell tower, is rung with light.

Some nights we see on your visage the features of man:
moonstone of your eye, lips like the crease you press into cloth.

Like the goat who springs from your head,
you are capacious, melody and milk.

From your shadows fall
polygons of light, clouds of bathing women.

In your belly is a man full grown, universe of one,
he looks out at us from his glass egg,

to which you point, you who hold the stitches of your silence
like the teeth in your head,

the blues and greens of bread gathered in the basket of your chest,
men adoring at your skirt's hem.

The farmer lets loose his blessing of grain,
the canaries sing your skirt's pattern to flower,

and, woman, yellow as clay, green as cheese,
stand on our checkered earth and make of it a pattern for your bed.

IV.

Bella's in blue over Iva and me! She's tall as the zenith. Her hands,
thick with farm work and heavy dough, fumble

over us like tassels of a prayer shawl, working us
to a fine wool and holding us, like sparrows, in her palms.

She is the air over Vitebsk, variegated blue and white,
stern as the chapel, broad as the barn,

clod-turned, water on agate, seam in the well, weight of the ax,
sun on the compost, burning wick, skin on the goat's milk.

She is the shiver of polygons on the edge of our matchstick bed,
lover of song, banjo of broken chords.

She holds in her hands, like slivers of glass, the moments of death
that pool in the cracks in the mirror over our tub.

She loves the bird in my face, the elephant of my body, my feet
like mismatched fish in the river of our sheets.

My heart is a box of mirrors, the floor a mosaic of fractals,
sheet music walls, kaleidoscope love.

She's lightning and irrigated fields, the hard-packed road,
the broadcloth we wear each day, all day, holding us in its chapped
	hands.

She spins us, like kite tails, like windmills, like silos of birdsong, and
fills us, like inkwells of blown glass, with the confetti of her lungs.

V.

It is here the Jews are buried, tomb-shack and dew,
where, as a child, Chagall sat

and saw the headstones crooked as teeth, broken
on the wind's ice chips, the sky disordered as cells

dividing in wild abandoned symmetry.
Homes built into the cemetery adhere, inebriated by danger:

a roof blown off, a slumping stairway, a whip-racked banister.
But slowly, from across the lawn, Chagall began to see this graveyard
        maw turn

upended keys, as from a piano smashed, each stone a key
which plays, as from a throat, its Hebraic script of notes

against the sky's unwashed silk, which breathes deep
of the sordid earth, inhales its broken chords,

so that he thought it almost possible that from the holy cow
strung, unsleeved, on the butcher's door, from that carnival of gore,

might rise in the steam of the newly killed something like sound, like
    thought
enhanced by shadow on the theater wall,

and that perhaps, as from these unhinged homes, the rubble stones, we
    escape,
he began to think, the body's domesticity for a sky both lightning-
    struck and mute.

VI.

Village of habits, of wood planks and barns,
village the pattern on the table's cloth,

lay yourself with Bordeaux and Brie,
light your candelabra of chimneys

with woodsmoke laced in spruce, snuff
from the pipes of old men, let your families come out

onto the hip of the earth, your chickens,
your goats, your three-headed men, for Uncle Neuch

jigs over Vitebsk tonight as he did,
once, at our weddings and funerals, though now

his face is spinach leaves, his violin's aria
umber and saffron, and across the sky's

hilltop, his pointed shoes imprint:
triangle, heel, triangle, heel.

Ladies, dance fat and furious in your big-print
dresses, for he jigs over the synagogue

and the one-eyed church, over
the starlings and chicken coops.

Come, come! For, love, he's come
from the grave to dance on our roof.

JOHN DONNE ON HIS DEATHBED

> . . . *As West and East*
> *in all flatt Maps (and I am one) are one,*
> *so death doth touch the Resurrection.*

You glistened like a baked and porous shoreline
so racked with chill, the trees threw their hair
in the sand, the canoes, though tightly lashed,
ricocheted in the dilated coverts of your arteries,
and your physicians, with a love
grown wild, examined each grit and follicle
as though it were a sign. *Be this,* you wrote,
slick with love, salted in dying, *my Text,*
my Sermon to mine own: the body as emblem
or prophet! O, mysterious oracle, that leads us
from this world into the next, by what science
do we decipher you, by what strange anatomy?
Within my inky aqueducts, electric fretwork,
cleft belfry of my heart, I hear your clangor.
Ring out, instead, the cool clear note Donne's
physicians heard as they bent to him in death,
who saw then the map of his body become globe,
the string of breath threaded through the loom
of his lungs become fabric, his westward passage opening
before him, the silvered Pacific, each physician
standing then, a little shattered,

his dram of spirits the color of stained glass.
In death's witching hour, what epistle
did you leave, what glassy bauble thrown
across the billowing of your sea-blue iris?
The ice-grip stop-clenching your heart's rondure,
by what surveyor's tool were your physicians
to chart, to some spangled crystalline zone,
your passage? By what distant sparkling
compasses did you proceed? Your mast lamp
swaying the ocean's flaxen membrane,
flux of your sextant's needle, broad barrel
of your progress, did you feel the suck
of a latitudinal defect, whirlpool of sea-flume,
or did you find then some new passage,
the strait you'd believed in your whole life
siphoning you, not—you realized then—like an explorer
to his newfound land, but like all the dead before you
swimming for the equinoctial provenance
through the damp pockets of their lungs?

NOTES

"Seasonal Incantation" draws inspiration from Galenic medicine, the leading medical model from ancient times up to the Renaissance, when the "new anatomists" rejected inherited book learning for an aggressive study of the body through dissection. This poem is very loosely based on a series of anonymous Galenic medical prints entitled "The Four Seasons of Human Life."

"The Artist at His Canvas" is based on Lucian Freud's painting *Painter Working, Reflection* (1993); "At the Salon of 1865" is based on Édouard Manet's *Olympia*; and "Hygieia" is based on a detail of the Goddess of Health from Gustav Klimt's *Medicine* (1900–1907).